OUT OF
CONTROL

OUT OF CONTROL

Rick *Jasper*

MINNEAPOLIS

Darby Creek
A division of Lerner Publishing Group, Inc.
241 First Avenue North
Minneapolis, MN 55401 U.S.A.

Website address: www.lernerbooks.com

The images in this book are used with the permission of:
© Kelpfish/Dreamstime.com, p. 109; © iStockphoto.com/
Jill Fromer, p. 112 (banner background); © iStockphoto.
com/Naphtalina, pp. 112, 113, 114 (brick wall background).
Front Cover: moodboard/CORBIS.
Back Cover: © Kelpfish/Dreamstime.com.

Main body text set in Janson Text 12/17.5.
Typeface provided by Adobe Systems.

Jasper, Rick, 1948–
      Out of control / by Rick Jasper.
         p.   cm. — (Travel team)
      ISBN 978–0–7613–8323–9 (lib. bdg. : alk. paper)
      [1. Baseball—Fiction.] I. Title.
   PZ7.J32Ou 2012
   [Fic]—dc23   2011027948

Manufactured in the United States of America
1—BP—12/31/11

*To my grandmother, who
bought me my first glove*

"The way a team plays as a whole determines its success. You may have the greatest bunch of individual stars in the world, but if they don't play together, the club won't be worth a dime."

—BABE RUTH

CHAPTER 1

*I*f you had attended the baseball game between
the Las Vegas Roadrunners and the Boise
Bulls on that steamy June afternoon, you would
have seen something unusual. Both summer
travel teams were at the elite level, which is
to say that both teams had teenage players
under seventeen years old with college or even
professional potential. But that afternoon you
would have seen something that looked more
like a scene from a Little League game.

It began simply enough. The Roadrunners were down by two in the bottom of the eighth inning. Thanks to a walk, they had a runner on first with nobody out: their shortstop, Carlos "Trip" Costas. Trip was speedy, so the expectation was that he would try to steal second, and indeed he was taking a generous enough lead to draw the attention of the pitcher.

The Bulls' pitcher was good enough, or well-coached enough, to expect the steal. But even if he had been unaware, the screaming of one of the Roadrunners' fans would have alerted him.

"STEAL! STEAL, CARLOS! Jeez, move your butt! This guy's got nothing!"

A few people in the crowd looked around, but most of the Roadrunners' faithful knew without looking that the screamer was Trip's father, Julio. Like Trip, they ignored him.

The game slowed down considerably with the next batter, center fielder Danny Manuel. He was a good match for the pitcher; both of them were—to put it nicely in a word often

used by sports broadcasters—"deliberate."
They took their time. The pitcher would fool
around with the resin bag, make a couple of
throws to first, fool around with his cap, and
then again go to the resin bag. Once he was
finally ready to pitch, Danny would call time
and step out of the batter's box.

When a pitch actually managed to occur,
Danny would foul it off. The afternoon
was warm, the sun was bright, and the sky
was a monotonous, cloudless, desert blue.
What should have been a tense situation was
becoming nap-inducing.

Julio was still awake, though. He was still
yelling for the steal. And he was still being
ignored, as the attention of the other fans and,
as it turned out, some of the players waned.
The count drowsed its way to 2–2, and Danny
kept fouling off pitches—over the backstop,
tipped into the dirt, down the line, high, low.
It was after about seven of these that the Bulls'
catcher noticed Trip's overlong lead.

The next pitch was outside, on the first-
base side of the plate. The catcher gunned

it to first and Trip, as he admitted later, was caught napping. The first baseman tagged him out, the Roadrunners' fans groaned, and Trip headed back to the dugout.

From the seats came an outraged bellow, and suddenly Julio was on the field, heading for his son. What transpired looked like a coach-umpire altercation, with Julio in the role of coach, cursing in Spanish and waving his arms, while Trip stared at him with little expression while trying to walk away. That's when the shoving started. Julio grabbed the teenager by the shoulder and started shaking him. Trip was four inches taller and pushed his dad away, but Julio kept grabbing him and getting in his face.

"What were you thinking? You had that guy! You could steal standing up!"

Finally, Trip started backing his dad up, shoving the heels of his hands against Julio's chest.

Before things got really ugly, the umpires converged on the two and the Roadrunners' bench emptied. The resulting spectacle consisted of a baseball team separating father from son, handing Julio over to security and shielding Trip as they ushered him to the dugout. Trip hadn't said anything to that point, but as his dad was escorted out he turned and yelled, in a voice as impressively loud as Julio's, "Happy freakin' Father's Day!"

When the game finally resumed, Danny flied out. Zack Waddell singled, but he was then thrown out on Nick Cosimo's subsequent grounder. The Roadrunners went quietly in the ninth and lost by two. But by then the game itself seemed like a sideshow to the main event. When people left the field that night they were talking not about who won or lost, but about crazy Julio Costas.

My father.

CHAPTER 2

Yes, my dad is *the* Julio Costas. Your parents probably have some of his records. Maybe they've even seen him perform in Vegas, where he pretty much stays now except for when he has TV appearances and recording sessions. He never liked touring, and now he doesn't need to.

Here's a description from Wikipedia:

Julio Costas is a Venezuelan singer who has sold over 200 million records worldwide in fourteen

*languages. He has released forty albums and is
one of the top twenty best-selling musical artists in
history. He became internationally known in the
early '80s as a performer of romantic ballads.*

His story is more interesting than that,
and he's very fond of telling it, so I know it by
heart. Dad was born in the La Dolorita barrio
of Caracas. He took me and my brothers on a
trip to Caracas once, but we didn't go near La
Dolorita. It would have been too dangerous.
The dream of the people who live in its violence
and dirt is to get out, but the options for escape
are limited. Some choose crime. A few with the
talent try sports, and that was Dad's dream.

Venezuelans are crazy about baseball, the
way Brazilians are crazy about soccer, and the
amateur leagues there have been attracting
major-league scouts for years. The country
produced a Hall of Famer in the '50s in
Chicago White Sox shortstop Luis Aparicio,
plus a lot of other stars along the way. Today
you could point to Bobby Abreu or Magglio
Ordonez or Carlos Zambrano. Anyway, Dad
also had talent. He's a lefty, and he could pitch.

By the time he was thirteen, baseball scouts had noticed him, but he'd also been noticed by a scout of another kind. Dad and a few of his buddies would make extra money singing on downtown street corners—traditional Latin stuff and songs from movies. One day a music executive named Domingo Villa stopped to listen, and he was sure he heard something special in Dad's voice. In two years, with Villa as his agent, Julio Costas had a bestselling album and an international tour, and the two men began to get rich together. Dad left baseball behind. Well, not entirely.

When he was twenty-five, my dad married his second wife, a nineteen-year-old Spanish tennis star who gave him three sons, my older brothers and me, before she and Dad split. I was only two when the divorce happened, but apparently there was some bitterness because she has never tried to involve herself with us. She married a Swiss doctor and is now raising a second family in Europe.

Meanwhile, Dad has married three more times, most recently a Vegas dancer seven years older than me. None of Dad's wives have really been "moms" to us, but it hasn't seemed like an issue. We've had nannies, Dad has always paid plenty of attention to us, and there's been baseball since we could walk.

Dad still dreams of sports glory, but now it's for his sons. So we've had private coaching, the best equipment money could buy, and constant encouragement. Well, "encouragement" is putting it mildly. Dad has always been pretty over-the-top about our working hard and succeeding in his favorite sport.

And, by and large, we've made him happy. My oldest brother Julio Jr. (J.T.) plays Triple-A in North Carolina, while Alex, the middle son, is getting attention as a catcher at UCLA. And Dad has the biggest ambitions of all for me. He thinks I'm the most athletically gifted of the three of us, and he wants results.

All three of us have played for the Roadrunners. In fact, Dad is probably the biggest financial backer of the team. He makes sure the team is what he calls a "class act."

We travel in comfort, and we stay at the best places when we're away. When we're at home, we have chartered time at a high-end gym and a part-time trainer to give individual attention to every team member.

It sounds like a great deal. But there's one problem. I am sick of baseball.

CHAPTER 3

I've been playing baseball almost every day for a dozen years. And not just playing— training and practicing too. When I'm not on a field, I'm looking at videos.

Even when we were really little, it was all about baseball. On Monday nights when Dad wasn't performing, he'd sit J.T., Alex, and me down in front of the screen in our home theater for ESPN *Monday Night Baseball.* He would turn off the sound because he had no patience for the broadcasters. And he would comment on every play himself. We had to be ready for questions.

"J.T., pay attention. Why is the outfield playing in?"

"Alex, how come that pitch got by the catcher?"

"Can you believe it, Trip? The guy threw to first! What was the right play?"

This wasn't all crap. Dad knows baseball. And the three of us, by the time we were ten, knew it too. We'd been lucky enough to have talent and training, and we were all grateful and eager to please Dad.

It wasn't until I was thirteen that I expected anything more out of life than becoming a major-league star. When I did, it was because of Dad. Next to baseball, the biggest thing in our house, naturally, was music. Musicians came to see Dad, to jam with him, all the time. These guys were millionaires whose names weren't known outside of the small print on album credits, but they were legendary instrumentalists sought out by vocal stars like my dad who knew their value.

Music was a different world from baseball. I don't mean to say there isn't creativity in sports, but baseball—and I would think most sports—is about dependability, repetition, and routine. There is no situation in baseball that hasn't happened before, and for every situation there's a time-tested, reliable strategy for handling it. But music is full of surprises. In music there are no "percentage plays." Genius gets to play. Doing the unexpected is a good thing. I feel like I've always known this.

When Dad and his friends played around, if I wasn't at baseball practice, I would find a place to listen. I picked up keyboard and guitar pretty early. I practiced whenever I had a chance. Kinda funny—you hear about kids wanting to bolt music lessons so they could play outside. I was the opposite.

A couple of years ago I even started a band with three guys I know at school. We call ourselves Four. Dad was okay with it as long as it didn't interfere with you-know-what. We do covers of pop stuff, and we've actually played at a few school dances and some parties.

But baseball was fun too. I thought my brothers were heroes, and I always expected to play for the Roadrunners. When I was old enough and realized Dad was right about my talent, I was happy in a kind of unthinking way. And I loved that Dad was happy about me.

So when did it all change? It wasn't clear-cut. I guess baseball just lost the element of surprise, and that was something I valued. The closer I got to choosing baseball as a profession, the more I started to feel closed in. Trapped. Everyone I talked to seemed to be talking about my future in baseball, like it was all decided. But I didn't decide. Shouldn't it be my decision? Maybe it was like an arranged marriage, and I was starting to feel like a runaway groom.

I still play and work at playing, even though my teammates and coaches sometimes tell me I don't look too aggressive at the plate. "You've got a good eye, though." Which means I walk a lot. Which means I score a lot. At shortstop—that's my position—I get recognized. Shortstop allows for most of the very limited creativity available in baseball. After the catcher, the shortstop is the playmaker.

There was this one game. We were ahead by one. The other team had runners on first and second with no outs. The batter slashed a grounder deep to my left—deep enough that the runner on second was off for third. There was a force at second, but the batter was speedy—no double play. So I'm going for the ball and out of the corner of my eye I see the base runner stumble a step on his way to third.

Our third baseman, Nellie Carville, is smart and powerful. The stumble happened, and I knew Nellie saw it too. When the ball got to me, I wheeled 180 degrees and gunned it to Nellie. His throw to second just nailed the guy sliding in. It was pretty. It was surprising. Was it genius? Probably not, but it made me happy.

That play, by then, was an exception. I was playing, but I wasn't looking forward to it. I could feel that something was wrong. I could feel some kind of pressure building. What would Dad say if I quit?

CHAPTER *4*

*I*f I really didn't know the answer to that question, I got it in the game on Father's Day. Dad's jumping onto the field to yell at me was really the climax of something that had been building for a while.

For example, I already missed two practices. I really did feel too sick to play those days, but I can't say part of it wasn't mental. And when I did play, even when I tried to concentrate, there were times when I wasn't all there.

Coach Washington, whom we all call Wash, was the first to notice. We were playing in Salt Lake City against a good team, the Salt Lake City Bobcats. In the second inning I picked up a routine double-play ball and threw to first instead of second. Gus Toomey was so surprised at first that he almost missed it.

Wash was on me as soon as I got back to the dugout. "What's up, Trip? Catchin' a few winks out there?"

In the seventh I batted second. Sammy Perez had walked ahead of me. We were a run up, but we needed more. On the first pitch I grounded into a double play. Wash was on me again: "Didn't you see the bunt signal? Wake up, man!" The fact was I missed the signal, but heck, I didn't need someone to tell me it was a bunt situation. My head just wasn't in it.

I know you've heard this exchange before:

Sportscaster to athlete: So, Joe, what's your team's plan for tonight's big game?

Athlete: We just want to go out there and have fun, Marv.

But I got to the point where baseball wasn't fun anymore. My automatic skills kept me in the lineup, but I was making more and more mental mistakes.

If Dad hadn't jumped onto the field when he did, he probably would have done it the night before. Luckily, though, he was doing a show then. Because I lost the game for the Runners.

We were a run up on the visitors in the top of the ninth inning, but our relief pitcher, Shotaro Mori, was struggling. By the time we had two outs, they had men on second and third.

The next guy up hit a very high fly to short left. I automatically yelled, "I got it!" and started back to catch it. "Automatically" was the problem. I was watching the ball but not listening to Darius McKay, our left fielder, who was coming up behind me, yelling, "Get out!"

In situations like this, the outfielder has priority over the infielder. Just to be sure, when two guys are calling for the ball like we were, the center fielder can yell "You!" to the guy who is supposed to get the ball. And Danny, our center fielder, was doing just that. It was Darius's ball, but all I was thinking was, "Catch it and the game's over."

At the last minute I heard Darius, and at the last minute I turned around and backed off. But Darius had seen that I was sleepwalking, figured what the heck, I'd catch it, and at the last minute he stopped coming in.

The result was two players looking at each other while the ball dropped between them. Since it was their last play of the game, both runners had taken off at the sound of the bat, and they both crossed the plate before Darius had even picked up the ball and tossed it to second.

The next batter grounded out to second. Wash didn't say a word when I got back to the dugout. Neither did Darius or Danny. It was Nellie, our captain, who came over to where I was sitting alone and sat down next to me. Just sat, without saying anything, but it meant something. I was grateful.

I held out hope that we would come back in the bottom of the inning, but we went down in order. Visitors 5, Runners 4. I should have felt terrible; I *did* feel terrible. But to be truthful, the bad feelings I had were only partly because I had let down the team. They were mostly because I just wanted to be out of there.

CHAPTER 5

After the Father's Day game where Dad lost it and got escorted off the field, Coach Harris asked me into the room he called his office. It was really just a big closet at the training facility with a desk and a couple of chairs. I was still feeling physically sick from adrenaline after the run-in with Dad. I didn't want to talk. To be completely honest, I was afraid if I did I might start crying.

Coach started, "Hey, Trip, I'm sorry about that. Is everything going to be okay at home tonight?"

"Sure, Coach. No worries," I said. Although I didn't really know what "okay," meant at that point.

"You know, I was talking to Wash," Coach continued. "There was a kid on the Phoenix Sand Demons. Really good. But last year he just . . . I don't know, he just started spacing out during games. He wasn't all there. We actually took advantage, started hitting it at him."

I knew who he was talking about, and my face started to burn. "Coach, you think I'm doing drugs?" Because that had been the case with the Sand Demons' player.

Coach was looking hard into my eyes. Then he looked away. "No," he said. "But Trip, you haven't been yourself this year. Is something going on?"

I wondered what would happen if I told him.

"I know your dad is . . . enthusiastic. Heck, he can push. Is that—?"

I decided to open up. "Coach, it's not my dad. He is who he is. It's me. I'm the problem. You say I haven't been myself. The fact is, I'm wanting so much to be myself. And right now baseball doesn't feel like part of that. It feels like a job."

Coach digested that. I expected him to say something like, "Relax. Just go out there and have fun." Instead, he said, "That happened to me. Except I was in my twenties, on track for the majors. And one day I just . . . didn't feel it."

"What did you do?"

"I tried to ignore it. I was good. There was a lot of pressure to perform, to move on to the next level. But I knew I needed some distance. So I asked my coach for a rest."

"What did he say?"

"Let's just say he didn't embrace it. I was valuable. But he was a good coach and an understanding man. I knew I mattered to him as a person more than a player. So he took me out of the lineup for a while."

"And . . . ?"

"After a few weeks I started caring about the game again. But in a different way. It's hard to explain."

"If you benched me, my dad would freak out completely."

"At me, not you."

"Let me think about it, Coach, okay?"

. . .

When I got home that night, Dad didn't seem to be around. I should explain our house. I guess it's called a villa, but it's big enough that people can be living there and you won't necessarily run into them. And we always had guests. I looked for Dad in the usual places—his office, the studio, the theater, the pool—but he wasn't there. So I went to my room, took a shower, and lay down with the TV on. *Sunday Night Baseball*. Shoot! In one of the breaks they reported on Dad's freak-out, complete with amateur video from someone in the seats. If Dad wasn't a celeb it wouldn't be news, but he was, and it was.

At eight o'clock I got a call from Coach Harris. A few minutes later there was a knock on my bedroom door. It was Dad.

"Come in, Dad."

"Trip, I'm sorry. I just . . ."

"Don't worry, Dad. You were right about the play."

"I didn't mean to embarrass you."

I looked at him for a moment. "You didn't, Dad. I love you. Don't worry."

"I'm too hard on you, you know? I'll back off. Just play, okay?"

"I won't be playing for a while, Dad."

"What do you mean?"

"I just got off the phone with Coach. He's benching me for a little while. He thinks I need a rest."

Dad's face and his tone of voice suddenly changed. "He what? Trip, the team needs you! That's crazy!"

"It's all right, Dad."

"Heck no it's not all right! I bankroll this team, and I don't back a loser! We'll see about Coach Harris."

"Dad, I want . . ."

But he was gone. I started to think about what he might do, what Coach would say, and it was just too much. I got my iPod going and filled my head with music. After a half hour or so I called Lisa.

CHAPTER 6

I met Lisa Mancini-Owens last year at, of all places, a Runners practice. Her granddad, Pop Mancini, supplies our team with all its gear. He owns three sports emporiums, called Pop's Stars Sporting Goods, in Las Vegas and its suburbs. Pop shows up at our workouts from time to time, and this one day he brought Lisa with him.

It turned out that she's just a year younger than me and, in fact, we go to the same high school. I learned this at the practice when she waved me over and introduced herself. We talked a little and I told her about Four, that we'd be playing a school dance in a week, and she said, "I know. I booked you."

Lisa was on the student council, which is why I didn't know her. Like any other huge high school, we've got jocks and student-council types and brains and a dozen other groups that seem to hang out pretty much with their own kind.

Anyway, that's how I met Lisa, and in a few months she was maybe my best friend. Not girlfriend. She's hot and all, but we just related more like brother and sister. We could talk about our stuff, any of it, and not feel like the other one was judging. She found out all about Dad and knew how I was feeling about baseball. She'd crack me up sometimes with her opinions about guys, and she shared personal stuff about her family and herself that she wouldn't tell anyone else. After a while, I learned that she wanted to play guitar, so I had started showing her how.

Anyway, I called her on the night of Father's Day when I couldn't sleep, and I told her everything that had happened. She just listened to the whole story without saying a word.

"Wow," she said when she was sure I was through. "Your dad is out of control." She thought for a few seconds. "You know, at least he said he was sorry. He loves you, I'm sure of that."

"Yeah, but he left here really mad."

"Do you think he'll make trouble?"

"It depends on whether he calms down. Sometimes after he loses his temper he gets embarrassed. Like the thing at the game this afternoon."

"I guess you can't do anything about that. How do you feel about being benched?"

"Honestly, I was relieved. Before that I was thinking of just quitting."

"My granddad likes your coach. And now I like him too. He's willing to take the heat for you."

"I just hate to cause him trouble."

"He's being a good coach. Let him do that. Sometimes the best thing you can do for someone is to accept their help, you know?"

She was right. Anyway, right now the ball wasn't in my court. Lisa and I talked a little more before I thanked her and turned in for the night.

. . .

The next morning Dad wasn't around. I had breakfast and drove my Lexus to our 9:00 A.M. practice. Everything seemed the same as usual, except neither Coach Harris nor Wash was there.

You don't always need a coach at practice. We all know the routine, and each group on the team has its own leader: Nellie for the infield, Nick for the pitchers and the other catcher, and Danny for the outfielders. Each group goes through its drills and then takes a turn in the batting cage. Still, it was unusual for Coach not to be there without telling us ahead of time.

We were just finishing up when he showed. He said hi to everyone as they passed but then waved me over. "Hey, Trip, got a second?"

"Sure, Coach. What's up?"

"Well, it seems that your father has been in touch with the team backers: Alexander Jamison, Pop Mancini, Gus Toomey's dad, and a few others."

"Oh yeah?" I had a sinking feeling in my stomach.

"He's threatened to withhold any funding to the team unless he gets what he wants."

"And he wants . . ."

Coach nodded. "You on the field. Or a new coach. Or else he says he'll take you and his money to another team."

I swore. "I'm not his property! I'm sorry, Coach. This is my fault. I'll . . ."

"Well, there's a kind of principle involved here. Can one person call the shots for everyone else, even if he does pay forty percent of the team's expenses?"

"Maybe I can talk to him?"

"It's okay for now, Trip. The other backers

want to talk about it, and Julio has given them until the weekend. Meanwhile, we'll proceed as planned. We have a game here on Wednesday, okay? I won't start you, but I'll use you if we need you."

"Okay, Coach." I was mad and sick. If Dad had been there I might have attacked him. I drove home prepared for a fight.

CHAPTER 7

I found Dad sunning by the pool with wife number five. They were stretched out motionless in swimsuits and sunglasses on adjoining chaise longues, frosty drinks on small tables at either side. I wondered if they were napping, but I walked up anyway and said, "Dad! We need to talk."

He didn't say anything at first, just waved me away with the back of his hand like you'd bat away a fly.

"I mean it, Dad."

"Later, Trip. As you can see, Ysabel and I are relaxing."

"Oh, it's all right, Julio," Ysabel said, sitting up. "I was going to have a swim anyway. Hello, Trip."

She got up, and Dad and I both watched her dive into the pool before speaking. Dad heaved a deep sigh. "Okay, son. What's on your mind?"

I told him what I'd heard. "Is that true, Dad? Because if it is, you're a jerk!"

"Well, the way you told it makes me sound unreasonable. And I'm not unreasonable. I only want what's best for the team, and for you."

"Can't you see that Coach is resting me because I'm burned out? I'm sick of baseball! I don't *want* to play!"

Dad's voice got harder. "Your playing or not playing is not up for discussion," he said. "You owe it to your team and your talent to play. Your coach is preventing that."

"Are you listening? Have you noticed that

I've been playing like crap lately?"

"Oh, I've noticed," Dad said, and now he sat up and pointed his finger at me. "You are getting lazy, Trip. Lazy! And I'm not going to let some so-called coach who wants his players to like him . . . I'm not going to let him help you to be lazy. When you play poorly, the answer is to play harder! Not to drop out. A coach should know that."

"Look, Dad, everyone can see that my playing baseball isn't about me, it's about you! You wanted to be a baseball star yourself, and now you're trying to live through your sons! But it's *my life* you're talking about. It's not yours!"

Dad was on his feet. "I gave you your life! Don't ever forget that."

"You're acting like a bully! Using your money for fists!"

Dad took a step towards me. "If I had ever spoken to my father the way you are speaking to me, he would have whipped me."

The next words just slipped out. "You didn't even know who your father was!" I was sorry almost as soon as I said it. It was true. In the slums of Caracas, Dad's mother had earned a living the only way she knew how. She was with many men, and young Julio had a succession of "stepfathers." But by saying it I had crossed a line.

Dad lunged at me. I stepped to one side and then wrapped my arms around him from behind. He struggled, but I was stronger, and he finally said, "All right! Let me go." He was breathing hard now. Then he turned to me and said, "You are a minor. I'm your parent. I will decide what is best for you, not what you think you would like. Now go."

"Look, Dad, I didn't mean . . ." But he gave me that backhanded dismissal wave again and headed to the pool to join Ysabel.

Do fights like this happen in every family? Maybe you only get that angry at the ones you love. At that moment, though, I felt like I'd broken something important, something I could never put back together.

CHAPTER 8

When I woke up the next morning it took me a moment to remember why I was feeling so sad. I thought maybe I'd try to find Dad, but I didn't see him around anywhere. By noon I was dressed in my uniform and driving to the field.

We were playing a team we knew well, the Carson City Capitals. If they televised games at our level, the Caps would probably get lots of airtime because of one player, their right fielder Bo "Beast" Bronsky. That dude is fun to watch if you want to see power.

The Beast is totally developed into his adult size, which is almost six and a half feet tall and around 240 pounds. One time I asked Carson Jamison, our pitcher, what it was like to pitch against Beast. He laughed.

"Embarrassing," he said. "If he catches one it's going to go a long way."

In fact, he'd had one measured last year at 456 feet.

"But you know," Carson went on, "he's a football player too. Hitting moving objects is what he's all about. It's like a reflex, so he's not disciplined. He strikes out a lot."

We didn't take the rest of the Capitals lightly, either. Tim Pesci was a fine hitter who batted right after Beast and drove in a lot of runs. And they had a lefty pitcher, Brian Groh, who was already getting scouted. He had three pitches—a wicked fastball, a slider, and a change. And he could locate all of them. Groh would be pitching against us today.

. . .

When I got to the dugout, Coach Harris looked totally focused on the game. You wouldn't have thought he had anything else on his mind. I did my best to follow his example, even though I wasn't in the lineup.

Coach had put Dave Teller, our utility man, in my spot at short. Dave is quiet, careful, and unspectacular in every way, but he is solid and consistent. He'd start with most of the other teams at our level.

A couple of guys came up when they saw the lineup. "Trip, you hurt?"

"Nah," I said. "Just getting a rest."

As the game got underway, it felt strange to be watching from the dugout. I thought I'd feel relief at not having to play; instead I just felt kind of antsy, like didn't have anything to do. Wash must have noticed, because he came over with his notebook and asked me to keep score.

On the very first pitch—Carson was on the mound—the Cap batter hit a high hopper to short. Dave let it play him. He caught it awkwardly close to his chest, and by the time he got a handle on the ball the runner was safe at first. It would have been a hard play for anyone to make, let alone someone who wasn't used to playing there.

The second batter struck out, and then the hoots and yells from the crowd started as Beast Bronsky came to the plate. He swung and missed at the first pitch, but the swing was like everything else about Beast: huge. You could almost imagine a breeze coming from the direction of home plate. But Carson handled him. Beast got under the 2–2 pitch and hit a mile-high fly to center. Danny could have made a phone call while he waited for it to come down.

Tim Pesci then hit a sharp grounder to short, and this time Dave handled it smoothly and tossed to second for the third out.

We came to bat, and it was clear right away that Brian Groh had his stuff. Darius got called out on a third strike. Gus popped to second. And Nellie—no Beast, but plenty powerful—fanned on three straight pitches. He came back to the dugout shaking his head and talking to himself: "Whoa, Nellie, slow down next time, okay?"

Carson held them in the second. Dave doubled in our half, but we left him stranded. When he came back in the guys said, "Nice hit, what did you do?"

Dave just laughed. "I have no idea."

It was shaping up to be a pitchers' duel when Beast led off the fourth. Carson tried to sneak a first-pitch fastball past him, but the big man was all over it. Everyone heard the metal clank of the bat, and the crowd began yelling. Carson didn't even look back to see how far it went. And Sammy in right didn't leave the spot where he was standing; he just turned around and watched it sail away. It was 1–0.

That was still the score in the top of the fifth, with two outs and the Caps' number-two hitter at the plate. A scary power hitter often makes life at the plate better for the guys who hit immediately before and after them.

Since power hitters get walked more often, the batters who follow them see men on base more often and have a better chance to do some damage.

The hitters right before the power guys, well, pitchers have extra incentive to throw them strikes. First, they don't want a guy on base in case the big man dings one. Second, with two outs—and this was the situation here—they can get out of the inning and avoid facing a Beast until the next inning, when he's guaranteed to come up with the bases empty.

So what I'm saying is Carson wanted the Caps' pre-Beast hitter out in a special way. He wasn't going to try fooling him with pitches off the plate and risk a walk. Unfortunately he missed his spot on one and the batter knew what to do with it, lining it just over the fence near the foul line in left. Beast struck out, but the damage was done, and we trailed 2–0.

There was no change until we came to bat in the bottom of the eighth. Then, like rainclouds on the horizon after a drought, we noticed signs that Brian Groh was tiring. He walked the first two batters. Carson was due at the plate, but Coach had already decided his day was done.

"Costas," he called down the bench. "You hit for Jamison."

I jumped up and grabbed a helmet and a bat, took a few practice swings and took my place in the batter's box. Since Groh had started tiring he was missing mostly high. I thought I had a good chance to walk like the others, but I was also looking for one that might stray to where I could hit it. On the third pitch, with a 2–0 count, I got it. A fastball up and over the plate.

It felt good when I hit it, but I didn't look up till I was near first, and I saw the ball rolling into the gap in left center. I made it into second standing up; both runners scored, and we were tied.

The Caps brought in a reliever, but our offense seemed to be rolling now. By the time we were out of the inning, we led 5–2. I played short for the ninth inning, while Shotaro came in to relieve the pitcher and retired the side in order.

Sweet, right? I should have felt great, but I didn't.

CHAPTER 9

*I*t just didn't matter to me. A lot of people, from what I hear, feel this way about their jobs. They do them, they perform in a responsible way, but part of them is just going through the motions, feeling trapped.

Trapped is what I felt like these days when it came to baseball. In every direction I looked, I was causing pain to people I cared about: my dad, my coach, my team. And all because I was tired of playing this game. It was so time for me to move on, but I didn't know how.

As I drove home, I searched my mind for something less gloomy to think about. Four! We had a gig Friday night, and we'd be practicing tomorrow. Whatever disaster the weekend brought, for the next couple of days I'd be doing something I loved. Dad was in avoidance mode, I guessed, and for now that was okay.

The band's job was at a sweet-sixteen party for Zoey Bouchay, a sophomore at our high school. Lisa knows Zoey. In fact, I think she helped us get the gig. What everyone knows— at least in Vegas, where "Show me the money" should be the city motto—is that Zoey is a Russian princess. My dad is rich, I admit. But Zoey's mom, well, she owned Bouchay Cosmetics.

"Expect celebrities," Lisa told me. "You'll be just one of about six bands. But everyone will be surprised at how good you are.

"It's weird, because Zoey should be completely spoiled. But she's a sweetheart.

A little embarrassed about the party, but her mom insisted."

Zoey's parents came from Russia in 1992 with cash. They started the cosmetics company, which went nuts. When Zoey's dad split in '99, there was plenty of money to go around. Anyway, the party was going to be an MTV-style bash. And Four was playing at it. This could really put us on the map.

Let me tell you about Four. I'm keyboard and vocals. We've got Manny Ruiz on drums, Ethan Davis on guitar, and Phil Terrier on bass. I don't mean to brag, but for our age and repertoire, we're good. No big-time recording ambitions. We just want to do the music right. That's what makes us a team.

I wish my dad could hear us, because we're like him that way. Pure. Dad's music may not be everyone's thing, but in listening to him, everyone does hear truth. His voice is great. It's pleasant, but there are a lot of those voices. Dad's singing is true. He believes in the lyrics. His signature song, in fact, he wrote himself. It went triple platinum or whatever, but he has to sing it now every time he performs.

It's called "The Dream I Left Behind."
The song has gone cultural.

> *I've loved the world, its women and its gold.*
> *I've had the life, but when I'm growing old*
> *I know one thing will haunt me:*
> *The dream I left behind.*

I'm pretty sure it's about baseball.

CHAPTER 10

The road to Zoey's place was already crowded when we drove over Friday night. Hummers, Escalades, and every model of Mercedes could be seen. Of course there was a gate at the entrance where security guards were checking invitations. It took us a half hour to get inside the villa, even though we were early.

We'd be playing out by the pool. All the sound equipment was provided. When it was our turn we'd just have to plug in. My bandmates were gawking at the estate. The main house was designed to look like a French country mansion, and to get to the front you drove around a tree-circled artificial lake dotted with fountains. To one side were garages and an acre of cobblestone where the guests could park, and it was already filling up. Valets circled around in golf carts, ferrying guests to the house.

Since we had equipment, the valet took us straight to the back. Beyond a huge expanse of lawn and trimmed hedges were the white marble columns that surrounded the *big* pool. The smaller one apparently was right behind the house. When Manny saw the pool he whistled. "Wow, man, this will be like playing in an arena!"

The bandstand was at the far end of the pool; the patio that surrounded the water was probably bigger than the parking lot, and all around it were tents and tables with things to eat and drink. Lisa had told me that Zoey's mom was totally strict about underage drinking; if you tried for the champagne you'd get carded. I wasn't tempted anyway—I'd had beer a couple of times and I didn't like the way it made me feel—but I'd seen parties get rowdy because of kids drinking and doing other stuff, and I was glad this wasn't going to be one of them. Assuming the adults behaved themselves.

We weren't going to play until around sunset—ten or so—so we put our stuff in a safe place and went looking around. As the crowd grew, we all saw kids we knew from high school. But most of the people here would be relatives or folks Zoey's mom, Nadia, knew. After half an hour I spotted Lisa, who was looking for us.

"Hey, Trip," she called, and then came over and gave each of us a hug. "Nice place, huh?" Manny's eyes were still big as he took in everything.

"Yeah," I said. "Any idea how many guests?"

"Three or four hundred invited, plus whoever they bring," Lisa said. "Come on up to the house. I want you to meet the birthday girl."

We followed a wavy marble path back across the lawn and entered the house through the back. A huge hall with a ceiling two stories high stretched straight through the house from front to back. Zoey and her mom were at the front, greeting guests. We walked up, and Lisa said, "Zoey, this is Trip Costas and his band." Zoey turned around, and I caught my breath. She was a green-eyed blonde, about my height, with a smile that left me, and I expect a lot of guys, tongue-tied.

"Hi Trip," she beamed. "Lisa talks about you all the time."

"Uh, happy birthday!" I said and introduced her to the guys. While I was searching for something clever, but not too clever to say next, her mother noticed us.

"Nadia," she said, and shook each of our hands. She had a heavy accent. "Trip, you're Julio's boy, aren't you?"

"Yes, ma'am."

"Well I can see his features, but you're taller."

"Yes, ma'am."

"Well," she said when she realized I was not good for much more than single syllables. "Make yourself at home. I'll look forward to hearing you fellows play."

Lisa put a hand on my shoulder as we all headed back to the pool. Leaning over, she whispered to me, "In case you're wondering, she doesn't have a boyfriend."

I looked at her mischievous grin and laughed. "You are hilarious, girl." But she was also smart. I *had* been wondering.

. . .

Celebrities. By the time were setting up I'd seen a dozen. I guess they were fans of Zoey— and the makeup line. Somebody said Justin Bieber was there, but I didn't see him. It was crowded around the pool, and the lights were turned on as the sun was setting.

Our set went well. There was a place where

people could dance if they wanted. But you could tell that a lot of them were just listening. That's what we wanted—for the sound to get people's attention.

For our last number we'd worked up something new. "Thank you," I said. "Our last song is special to me because it was written by my father. I hope you'll like what we've done with it."

Dad's version has a full orchestra—more than full, it's got about a million strings—and a bunch of dramatic high notes. We started it a little more up-tempo, but we let the wistful melody do its thing. What I'd added was a short guitar solo after "I know one thing will haunt me": a few bars based on a Venezuelan folk song Dad used to sing to us when we were little. It slows things down, and there really is something haunting about it, before I speak the last line without any accompaniment: "The dream I left behind."

It worked. There was a second of silence before the applause started, and we were saying our final thank-you when I noticed one of the guests who wasn't applauding, just looking at me with an expression I couldn't read: my dad.

CHAPTER *11*

The party, I'm told, went a lot later than a sixteen-year-old usually gets to stay up. We didn't stay long, though. After we played I couldn't find Dad, but Zoey came up with Lisa.

"Thank you," she said to all of us. "That last song," she touched my shoulder lightly, "it made me cry. In a good way."

On the way home, my head was spinning. Zoey, Dad, and the deadline Coach said he'd set for the weekend: play Trip or fire the coach or I'll throw the team into money trouble. When I got to our house there was still no sign of Dad. So I went to my room and wrote him a letter. I put it on the desk in his office; that was always the first place he went in the morning.

Dad,

First, I'm sorry about what I said when we had our fight by the pool. I wish you could hear how I feel about baseball right now without taking it personally. Right now I'm making mistakes on the field because I'm bored, burned out. My mind wanders away from the game.

A lot of times it wanders to music. I saw you at the party last night, and I wonder what you thought of the band. I wonder what you thought about our cover of your song.

Please talk with me about all this. Don't hurt Coach or the team because you're mad at me.

Trip

• • •

When I got up the next morning, my head was still buzzing. We had a practice scheduled. There was a local game on Sunday, and then next week the Runners were flying to the Beach Blowout, a big tournament in San Diego. I went to the breakfast room, but Dad wasn't there. I made some toast in the kitchen and was going to get milk when I saw an envelope with my name on it taped to the refrigerator door.

Trip,

I'm sorry too about our fight. We both have Latin tempers.

I don't want to hurt Coach Harris or the team. But I have a son with special gifts, and if I let him waste those gifts I am failing as a father. The best thing for you right now is to play through your difficulties. That's best for your team as well. Taking your skills away from them because you are "bored" is self-centered.

You seem to think I am using my money as some kind of unfair power. In fact all the power is yours. All you have to do is play baseball the way

you always have, and all the problems you are
worried about will go away.

I'll be at practice today. I have a surprise for
you.

Dad

P.S. I was touched that your band played my
song. Thank you.

I was really confused. I loved my dad and
my team. But I was sure that the despair I
was feeling about baseball was more than just
selfishness. Was Dad saying, "Just go through
the motions, even though you want to be a
hundred miles away?" That wasn't like him.
We had more in common than our tempers:
we were both perfectionists. And playing
without caring was a kind of betrayal—of my
team, of my coach, and of myself. I was glad
Dad and I were communicating, even if it
was by letter. But his note proved that he still
didn't get it.

And what was the surprise?

CHAPTER *12*

When I arrived at practice, Dad was in the parking lot with a youngish guy who looked like he'd stepped out of a *GQ* article on "How to Dress for Watching the Game." Blue-and-white-striped silk shirt, chinos, Italian loafers, and a very expensive watch—*Patek* something. He had thick black hair cut short and a genuine tan. He also had Ray-Bans in his shirt pocket.

Dad waved me over. He was beaming.

"Brian," he said to the guy, "this is my son Trip. Trip, this is my good friend Brian Muller." We shook hands.

"Brian wants to watch you practice," Dad said. "He represents the New York Yankees organization, and he'll be at the game tomorrow as well."

What? The Yankees? Dad had gone nuts. Maybe this would have excited some guys. But to me it looked like a trap. Like being forced to date someone you didn't like just to please a parent. Except this was more than a date my dad was trying to arrange. It was my life. I felt like throwing up.

Another guy came over. He was younger than Brian, but he looked like he was taking his fashion lessons from the boss. I learned that he would be helping Brian "observe" the practice.

I didn't want to embarrass Dad. So I said, "Great," to the Yankees' guys. "Thanks!"

Right then I made a decision. I still can't be positive it was the right thing to do. But I was angry at Dad's manipulation. I was going to convince the scouts that I was no one they would be interested in.

. . .

I dogged it on the workouts. I let a lot of balls get by me. In the batting cage I tried to look clueless.

When I came out of the cage I just about collided with Dad. "What in God's world do you think you're doing?" he hissed.

"Dad, you still don't understand, do you? I don't want to give my life to baseball. Right now, I don't even want to play."

Dad's voice got cold. "You will play tomorrow. Your coach has agreed. You let me down today, but I know you will not let down your team."

After practice I found Coach.

"Dad said you'll play me tomorrow."

"Those are my orders, from all the backers," Coach said. "They want to cooperate with your dad, and he has said they'll have more time to negotiate if you play in the meantime."

"You do whatever they say?"

"Trip, I have to think about the whole team. Without your dad's support, our season might end. That's twenty kids, some of them with nothing in their life except baseball, who would be left with no season. And what was that from you today? Was that on purpose?"

"I wanted to chase Dad's scouts."

"Trip, I completely understand. If I was your dad, I'd tell you to take a break. But I'm not. I think honesty is the best policy. I'll do what I can; you do what you can."

. . .

In less than twenty-four hours the Runners would be meeting the South Denver Miners. We usually beat them, but word was they had a new pitcher—a knuckleballer. Following the majors, it's easy to think of a knuckleball as something a pitcher develops because he's getting older or just doesn't quite have the stuff of the competition.

Of course the rare knucklers that exist in the majors are, well, the best. But a few amateurs do work on that pitch, and word was that Dewey Wilkins, the new guy for the Miners, had one of the best at our level.

The fact that I was even thinking about this now proved that Dad had me pegged. I didn't want to let down the team. So I would play. And I made up my mind to play as well and as hard as I could, because I'd decided this would be my last game.

CHAPTER *13*

On the day of the game, Wash gave us a little talk on how to hit a knuckleball. None of us had ever before seen one in a game.

"My grandfather threw a knuckleball in the Negro Leagues," he told us. "He called it his 'butterfly' pitch. He used to say the knuckler is hard to hit because you don't know where it's going. But neither does the pitcher. The ball could accidentally wind up right where you want it."

Wash grabbed a bat and took a stance. "The first thing is to move up in the box a little. You'll give the pitch less time to move around. The next thing is to be patient. The knuckler comes in slow, so wait on it and watch it as long as you can.

"When you're ready to swing don't look up. Watch the ball hit the bat."

Carson was on the mound for us. As we got started, I spotted Dad and the Yankees' guys in the seats off the third baseline.

The first batter grounded to second for out one. Carson walked the next guy. The umpire wasn't giving him much on the low side of the strike zone, and that might mean trouble. Carson's fastball has a natural sink to it, and he gets batters to hit a lot of ground balls.

That's what happened with the next hitter. He hit the ball hard on the ground to my left. I caught it on the run and flipped it to Zack, who turned the double play. I could hear Dad yelling his approval from the stands.

Dewey Wilkins took the hill in the bottom of the inning. The Miners' catcher was wearing a mitt the size of a trashcan lid. Darius was up first, and frankly, he looked a little silly trying to hit the ball. After he struck out, he came back shaking his head. I heard Wash say, "Be patient."

Gus actually made contact with the ball, hitting a high foul behind the plate that the catcher grabbed. Nellie, our power hitter, got the count to 3–2, but he fanned on a pitch that wound up in the dirt. It looked like Wilkins had his stuff.

Carson retired the side in the second. Sammy was first up for our side and actually hit the ball, but he was underneath it and flied out to short right field. I was up next.

I was thinking about holding back and being patient—all the stuff Wash had said—so I didn't even swing when Wilkins threw a nice, fat fastball right down the middle on the first pitch. Man! Even knuckleballers mix in a fastball or a curve now and then, just to keep the batter off balance, in case he wasn't that way already.

The next pitch was outside. I took it, but I really hadn't seen it. It could just as easily have wound up a strike. In other words, the pitcher was still controlling me. The next pitch I swung at and felt nothing but air. It looked like it was going to be a short day.

Wilkins's next delivery looked like a ball, but it fluttered over the plate at the last minute, and I knew I'd struck out. I heard the umpire yell strike, but then I heard the fans yelling. The ball had gotten away from the catcher, who was chasing it to the backstop. By the time he found a handle on it I was standing on first base.

Danny was at the plate after me. I was taking a big lead, trying to distract the pitcher. The fact is, stealing second on a knuckleballer is easier than with other pitchers: the ball takes longer to get to the plate, and it's harder for the catcher to handle.

Wilkins had plenty of experience with that, but he wasn't about to give me a free pass. He threw over to first a couple of times. I'd dive back, but I kept the long lead.

I think what happened next was Wilkins trying to get me out by way of the catcher.

In any case, he threw a fastball. I broke for second, but it didn't matter. The fastball was outside, but not far enough. Danny's a righty, and he stepped into the pitch and parked it over the fence in right. We were two up.

The Miners got one back in the fourth on two doubles, but our hitters were starting to see the knuckleball a little better. The second time around the order three of us got hits, one of them mine, even though we didn't score.

In the eighth they touched Carson. The first two batters singled and were standing on the corners. The third guy then hit a fly to shallow left. I yelled for it and started back, but then I heard Darius yelling, "Get out!" I wasn't going to make this mistake twice, so I gave way.

Somehow, though, Darius dropped it. As he was running in, it hit his glove and bounced in front of him, so he booted it towards me. We were lucky in a way. The runners had held up in case it was caught, and the guy on third had only average speed. I barehanded the kick from Darius and gunned it to the plate from the grass in left. The throw was on the money, no hops, and Nick tagged out the runner.

Dad was again going crazy, slapping Brian on the back and yelling, "Heck of a throw, Trip!" There was a time when Dad's approval would have meant the world to me. Now it just left me cold.

CHAPTER *14*

I came to the plate first in the bottom of the eighth with the score 2–1. Maybe Wilkins thought I'd forgotten about the previous times I'd batted. But he tried first-pitch fastball again and this time I nailed it, a long liner to the gap in left center.

I'm not quite the fastest runner on the team in a straightaway. That would be Darius McKay. On the bases though—well, that's one of my strengths. By the time the throw came in from the outfield I was standing on third.

That woke up Wilkins, who struck out our next batter. Then Nick stepped in, called time, stepped out and tapped the bat against his left shoe, like he was knocking dirt off his spikes. What he was really doing was sending a signal: suicide squeeze. I was going to go on the pitch, and Nick was going to bunt.

The biggest thing that could go wrong was Nick missing the ball. I'd be caught— hence the name "suicide." And trying to bunt a knuckleball is risky, for obvious reasons. But I guess Coach was feeling frisky, and the Miners were asleep.

At the second Wilkins passed the point of no return in his windup, I was off. Nick squared away and put down a bunt that was beautiful enough to make you cry: a slow roller that hugged the line so close I skipped over it on my way in to score. There wasn't even a throw. The Miners knew they'd been had. It was 3–1.

Coach pinch-hit for Carson, but Dave Teller hit into a double play and the inning was over. All we needed were three outs from Shotaro. But as luck would have it, the first Miner up homered and the second one singled. The next scene was a common one on our team, though. Nick would go out to Shotaro and say some magic words—we never knew what they were—and Sho would settle in. He struck out the next batter and got the one after that to ground into a double play.

Okay, I was really, really tired of baseball. But even so, a game like this one was a lot of fun. And good times like this are best of all when a bunch of guys is sharing them. It reminded me of the way I used to feel before "my baseball future" became so serious.

Dad was out in the parking lot with the Yankees' scouts, grinning and waving me over.

"Haven't I been telling you, Trip? You've got what it takes! Great game!"

Brian nodded in agreement. "Nice work, Trip. The way you turned that blooper into an out at home, that was great."

"We're going to be in San Diego at the Beach Blowout later this week," the other scout said. "We're looking forward to seeing you play some more."

I just said, "Thanks."

"I'm taking my friends out for a while," Dad said, "but I'll see you at home later, okay?"

"Sure," I said. But I lied.

CHAPTER *15*

I drove home, knowing Dad wouldn't be there, and packed a few things. Then I called Lisa.

"Hey, Lisa," I said when she answered, "I need a favor."

"Name it," she said.

"I need a place to hang out for awhile. Do you have a spare room?"

"Sure, you can use the guest room. What's up?"

"Same old. Baseball. My dad. I'll tell you more when I get there."

Lisa's place wasn't a villa, but it was nice. Her mom was Pop Mancini's youngest daughter who, like most of the family, went into the family business. But Lisa's mom had also gone to medical school and wound up as a psychiatrist. Being a psychiatrist in Vegas is like being a blanket salesperson in Alaska. There's a need.

Lisa came to the door when I rang and welcomed me in. "Is this okay with your parents?" I asked.

"They're out of town till next weekend," she said, "but they'd be cool. I'll show you your room."

After I got settled we sat down in the rec room and played some video games. Lisa didn't ask any questions; she knew I'd talk when I was ready. And I did, after an hour or so. I told her about my argument with Dad, his blackmailing me and the team, the Yankee scouts—everything.

"I just want to get away," I said. "From him and his expectations."

Lisa was quiet for a minute. "So," she asked, "is it really baseball you hate, or is it the way it's turned into something about your dad?"

"Wow," I said, and smiled at her. "How soon until you join your mom's practice?"

She laughed. "Really, Trip, maybe it's not baseball you want to get away from after all. Maybe your dad is just too involved for it to be fun anymore."

I thought about today's game and how great I'd felt when we'd won. Lisa was right. It wasn't the sport. When I thought about quitting, I was really thinking about how great it would be to not have to measure up to anyone's dreams but mine.

Lisa went on. "What's your plan? I mean, you can't really change your name and work construction in Canada. Sooner or later your dad will come looking for you. You'll have to go back."

"You're right, Li. I don't have a plan. I think I just need some oxygen for a while."

"We have oxygen here," she laughed. "Stay

as long as you like. I do have another guest tonight, though."

"I'm sorry, I didn't—"

"It's all right. The more the merrier. Plus you've met her."

That's how, later that night, I came to be sharing pizza and ice cream and movies with Lisa and Zoey. Dad had started calling around six, but I turned off my phone. And he wouldn't find me here; he didn't know anything about Lisa.

. . .

It was great. For four or five hours, past midnight, no one said the word *baseball*. And Zoey turned out to be almost as funny as Lisa. I laughed a lot that night. At some point we said good night—Zoey was sharing Lisa's room—and I went to the guest room for the best sleep I could remember.

The next morning I went out to their pool and swam some laps. We had a practice scheduled for that day, but I had no plans to go. After swimming, I cleaned up and wandered out to the kitchen, where Lisa and Zoey were cooking bacon and eggs and giggling.

"Hey, Trip," Lisa said. "Zoey dreamed about you."

The sixteen-year-old blushed and punched her friend in the arm. "Lisa!"

Lisa laughed hard. "Tell him about it."

Zoey rolled her eyes. "Actually," she was talking to me now, "it was kind of weird. You were singing that song your dad wrote—the one you sang at my party?—and then your dad came up and started singing too."

"I'll bet we made beautiful music," I said kind of sarcastically.

"No! You had different styles and you sounded terrible together. And you kept looking at each other like 'Stop already!' And you said, 'I was singing first,' and he said, 'I wrote the song.' I thought you were going to fight."

"What happened?"

"Dunno. I woke up."

Lisa was smirking. "Zoey, I think you may be a psychic. You are definitely in touch with the energy around here."

We ate breakfast. I checked my phone. There were lots of missed calls from Dad. I didn't want him to have a heart attack worrying, so I texted him. *Spent the night with friends. I'm fine.*

OK, he texted back, *see you at practice.*

I didn't answer.

. . .

Lisa and Zoey were planning to go to the mall that morning. I passed on their invitation. I thought I'd just chill by the pool, play games, whatever. I felt like I was on vacation—a vacation I'd needed for a couple of years.

The girls had been gone for just half an hour when the front doorbell rang. I looked out through a window and the old sick feeling started again. It was Pop Mancini.

CHAPTER *16*

I opened the door, and once again the world of baseball entered my life.

"Trip!" Pop said when he saw me. He seemed surprised, but friendly. I explained that I'd been visiting Lisa, and that she and Zoey had gone shopping.

"You were wise to stay home," he laughed. "They'll be hours."

He looked at me for a minute and said, "Sit with me by the pool. I think there's some lemonade in the fridge . . . Yep. Grab a couple of glasses."

So we headed out to the patio. It was a gorgeous morning, cool for the summer. We didn't say anything for a few minutes. Then he said, "Great game against the Miners."

"Yeah, it was."

"I meant you. You played great."

"Thanks."

"Scott Harris told me you're sort of tired of the game lately. That he wanted to give you a rest."

"Yes, sir."

"Apparently not what your dad had in mind."

"No, sir."

"Well, he talked to some of us about it. Said he'd pull his money out of the team if Scott didn't put you in the lineup."

"I heard that, sir."

"Call me Pop. You know, we kind of laughed at him. I mean he's very generous, but several of us have means."

"So the season wouldn't end if he . . ."

"Oh no. I think Scott was worried about that for a while. But we're all interested in keeping the Runners going." He looked at me. "And in taking care of our players." He paused a few seconds.

"Anyway, I talked to Coach this morning and told him to do what he thinks is best."

"Dad will freak if I don't play."

"Trip, I know you're the one who has to deal with him, but his 'freaking' won't affect the Roadrunners. And the Roadrunners do need you—you're a great player. But we need you healthy. Anyway, your dad won't know until Coach actually benches you. Right now he's assuming he's won, that you'll be in the lineup."

His cell phone rang. "Excuse me," he said, and then, "Yeah, it's not locked. Come on in."

A minute later the door to the patio opened and in came Wash.

"Hey Trip!" Wash said. "Thought we'd have little chat about your situation."

I looked at Pop. "You knew I was here?"

He smiled. "A friend of yours told me."

Lisa!

Wash tells stories, and of course he had one relating to my predicament.

"Trip, I played on a team with a guy— fantastic, could have made the MLB. And he loved baseball when he played. Who doesn't love doing something they're terrific at? But he had different plans for his life. He went to law school, and now he's in St. Louis defending people who can't afford a lawyer. He's happy with the past and happy with the present because he did the job he wanted to do when he wanted to do it. Once it was baseball. Now it's law. But he's the same guy, loving to do something he's good at."

I nodded. But Pop and Wash coming over to talk to me sort of blew me away. I couldn't get a word out of my mouth.

"Come to practice today, okay?" Wash said. "Have fun. If we get to San Diego and you feel like sitting, that's fine. We just want you with us."

"Sure," I said. "Thank you."

Pop said, "Do you need anything? I'll be at the practice."

"No, thanks, Pop. I'll pick up my stuff at home."

"I know what you're thinking, Trip," Pop said. "There's still your dad. He's very proud of you, you know?

"He thinks that pushing you is his duty. Heck," Pop laughed, "he thinks that pushing *everyone* is his duty. But you're growing up into your own person. Julio's going to have some trouble with that. I did. I was not happy with idea of my youngest daughter—who was a very talented softball player, by the way—I was not happy with her deciding she wanted to be a shrink. Today I'm very proud of her."

All in time, maybe. But right now the idea of seeing Dad at practice, with his current Yankee obsession, made me a little sick. If I had known what would happen in a few hours, I would have felt even worse.

CHAPTER *17*

I drove home and got my stuff, then drove to the field. I was hardly out of the car when I heard Dad's voice calling me from across the lot. He was all smiles.

"This is going to be a tough practice," he said. "You'll all need to be at the top of your game in San Diego."

He was right about that. The Beach Blowout was an invitational, and the best teams from the United States, Mexico, and the

Caribbean would be there. Just to be included was special.

We ran a few laps, stretched, and started our various warm-ups. We usually had a few spectators at our workouts. Some were parents of team members. Sometimes there were college scouts. And always there were a few kids or old people with time on their hands who just wanted to see some good players. Hardcore guys like Dad and Pop Mancini came whenever they could.

When my brothers and I were little, Dad actually helped coach some of our teams. Unfortunately, as we grew up, he never completely kicked the habit. It was pretty common for him to wander down on the field and ask the coaches questions—or even offer advice. Mostly Coach and Wash humored him; he did know baseball, and he cared about the team's success.

I was waiting my turn for batting practice when I noticed him jawing with Wash down by the dugout. He had on a glove, and he was demonstrating something with it while Wash nodded his head and smiled tolerantly.

Shotaro was throwing B.P. when my turn came. I started slow, trying to get down my timing. When I started hitting line drives I picked up the power a little. We always had a little fun seeing who could hit the farthest or put the most pitches over fence. The little kids would hang out on the other side with their gloves, shagging the balls that left the park.

I was just about at the end of my turn, so I thought I'd try to rip one really hard. That's something any batting coach from Pee Wees up will tell you is counterproductive. But I didn't care. I jumped on Shotaro's pitch way too soon and hooked a screaming liner right at the third-base dugout. I heard a shout and turned just in time to see the ball hit Dad in the head right above his left eye.

He dropped straight to the ground as Wash tried to break his fall. People, including me, came running from all directions. Somebody was yelling, "Call 911!"

The next twenty minutes seemed like hours. Dad was on his back, completely unconscious. He was breathing, you could see that, but blood was coming from a nasty gash on his temple and his face was starting to swell. Wash knelt beside him with a damp towel and wiped away some of the blood. I got down next to him and said, "Dad! Can you hear me?" But he didn't move.

At some point I began hearing sirens in the distance, and before long paramedics were bent over him, attaching wires and pushing open his eyelids to check his pupils.

"I'm his son," I said to one of the medics. "How is he?"

"His heart and breathing are good," he said. "He's got a head injury, pretty obviously. No telling how serious. We need to get him to the hospital."

"I'll follow you," I said.

"I'll go with you," someone said. I looked around. It was Pop Mancini.

"Me too," Nellie said.

They put Dad on a gurney and wheeled him out to the ambulance in the parking lot. With their siren screaming, they pulled out into traffic with the three of us right behind.

"I can't believe this," I said. "What if I killed him?"

"Don't start down that road, Trip," Pop said. "It wasn't your fault."

"Yeah," Nellie chimed in, "it was an accident. It could have hit anyone. Or no one."

I pulled into the emergency room entrance behind the ambulance. "You can get out here," Pop said. "We'll park the car and find you."

I jumped out and almost ran into a blonde woman with a microphone. Behind her was a guy with a video camera. "KLAS Channel 8," she said. "Is Julio Costas in that ambulance? What happened? Is it true he's in a coma?"

They were wheeling Dad into the hospital when the KTNV truck pulled up. I just followed the gurney, ignoring voices behind calling, "Mr. Costas! Wait!"

Wait is what I would do for the next six hours.

CHAPTER 18

Pop and Nellie caught up with me in the waiting room.

"So this is what it's like to be a celebrity!" Nellie said. "There were cops at the door to keep the TV guys from crashing the hospital."

A half hour later Lisa came through the doors. "Hey, Trip," she said and gave me a hug. "How are you doing?"

"I guess the question is 'How is *he* doing?'" I said.

"Not to me," Lisa shot back and put an arm on my shoulder.

We had probably been there about two hours when a guy in blue scrubs with blood all over them came out of the ER. His nametag said *Chris Williams, M.D.*, and underneath that *Neurosurgery.*

"Costas?" he said, looking around. I waved.

"Is Julio Costas your father?"

"That's right."

"I'm Dr. Williams. The EMT said your father was hit by a baseball, right?"

I nodded.

"He's still unconscious, but his vital signs are good. We x-rayed his skull, and he doesn't seem to have any fractures. So right now he's up in radiology getting a CT scan, so we'll know what's happening with his brain. I'll check back as soon as I have something more to tell you. Okay?"

"Yeah. Thanks. Is he going to live?"

"So far I don't see why not. What we'd be worried about is any bleeding or swelling in his brain. The CT will give us a lot more information."

After another hour I finally said, "Guys, Lisa, this could be a long time. You don't have to . . ."

They just looked at me and shook their heads. "Forget it," Lisa said.

. . .

Around hour four Dr. Williams reappeared. "Sorry to keep you waiting," he said. "This place is crazy tonight. The CT scan on your father was negative. He probably has a concussion, but with rest he'll be better in a while as long as he takes it easy."

"So he's conscious?"

"Getting there. He's coming to very slowly."

"Can I see him?"

The doctor looked at his watch. "Give him about two more hours. He's in a private room and resting comfortably, but we want to keep an eye on him a little bit longer."

Exactly two hours later I was at Dad's bedside. He reached his arms up as far as he could without straining the IV tube, and we hugged. He had a bandage on his forehead where he'd been hit and the beginnings of a black eye. But he was smiling.

"How are you feeling, Dad?" I asked.

"I'm fine," he said. "No one should know better than you what a hard head I have. You know, the last thing I remember was standing by the dugout talking to Wash. What really happened?"

I told him that someone at batting practice had pulled the ball and it had hit him.

"Do you know who hit it?" he asked.

"It was me, Dad."

He looked at me for a moment, and then suddenly laughed so hard I was afraid he'd hurt himself.

"Isn't that something?" he said. "After all we've been through lately?" Then he got serious. "Look, son, I need to tell you I'm sorry."

"Why? I was the one who—"

He held up a hand. "When I started to get my senses back, I don't know, instead of being in a fog it was like I was seeing more clearly than ever. And I saw an old man who was trying to turn his son into himself."

"What do you mean, Dad?"

"Trip, you told me over and over that you were tired of baseball. And I just wouldn't hear it. It was my way or the highway, right?"

"It's okay, I . . ."

"I was not respecting you, Trip. You are old enough now to make some decisions about your life, your future. I'm proud of you, Trip, baseball or not."

I didn't know what to say. But he went on.

"So I'll keep supporting the Runners. Coach Harris knows what he's doing. Between the two of you, you can decide whether you play."

"Thanks, Dad. I'm proud of you too, you know." We hugged again.

"You know," he said with a smile, "you're a pretty good singer."

CHAPTER 19

*D*ad wasn't going to make the trip to San Diego. He would be two more days in the hospital and had strict orders to rest at home for at least a week after that. No shows. No strenuous exercise. I felt sort of guilty leaving Dad behind, but Lisa promised to keep an eye on him. Turns out the two of them got along pretty well.

On Wednesday the Runners got on a bus and headed to the coast for the Beach Blowout.

We were about halfway there when Coach Harris came back to where I was sitting.

"What do you think, Trip? Do you want me to start Dave Teller at short?"

"I know you probably think I'm nuts, Coach," I said. "But I want to play." Lisa had been right. I didn't hate baseball. I just hated the expectation that baseball was my one and only future. As long as I was playing for the fun of it, and for the team, it was great.

Coach raised his eyebrows a little. "You're sure?"

I was.

As usual, the Runners had the classiest accommodations available. We were staying at a resort on the ocean in La Jolla, on San Diego's north side. We opened Wednesday night against the Phoenix Desert Eagles, an old rival. We were the designated home team in that first game.

Standing at shortstop, with the weight of Dad's dreams off my shoulders, I felt my focus return. My mind was sharp, my body felt fit, and I was excited to play.

• • •

We cleaned out the Eagles. There are times,
for all teams, when everything seems to be
working. You hope those times will happen
when they matter most. This was the biggest
tournament we'd played all year. There would
be only one bigger contest, the Elite Series
at the end of August, and a good showing at
the Blowout would probably get us invited to
that one. And that first night, we were stellar.
Every one of us. Nellie homered twice; Nick
threw out three runners at second; Danny was
so spectacular in center that he didn't look like
a show-off; Sammy doubled twice and stole a
base; Carson struck out ten; and I was three
for four and made one stab that had people
standing up to cheer.

The Force was with us as the week went
on. By Saturday we had only one game to
win in order to reach the championship on
Sunday. We played Los Lobos de Guadalajara,
a Mexican team that boasted four alumni of a
Little League World Series Champion team.

A big variable at our level, where guys are still teenagers, is physical development. We've all got skills, but we're still growing, so the guys who've developed more have an advantage. Los Lobos—that's The Wolves— looked, most of them, like adults. Not tall, necessarily, but bearded and muscular. Nick joked that half of them were probably married with children. And they played like they were earning their living at baseball.

Coach was resting Carson for the finals, if we made them, so he started Travis Melko. Travis pitched relief sometimes and started sometimes. He had three good pitches, none of them overpowering, but he had mad control and was a smart pitcher.

Travis's strength was also his weakness, though. The control that made him so effective sometimes deserted him. But I shouldn't have worried. That semifinal night, Travis pitched like a champ. The Runners homered three times—one was mine—and Travis shut out the Wolves on five hits.

CHAPTER 20

The final on Sunday night was carried by local TV stations on the West Coast, including Vegas. *Great!* I thought, because I hoped Dad would be able to watch. But Sunday morning he called me to say he was on his way to San Diego.

"Dad, you're supposed to rest!"

"I am resting, Trip. I'm using the chauffeur, and Pop Mancini's granddaughter is riding down with me. We're on the road right now."

"Lisa? Can she talk?"

"Yo, Trip! Can't wait to see you!"

"You amaze me, Lisa. Is Dad okay?"

"Now there's a question with a complicated answer," she laughed. "But healthwise, he's doing great."

"All right. See you tonight. Thanks!"

The final pitted the Roadrunners of Las Vegas against the Seattle Tide. Not a team we knew, and they didn't know us.

In the bus on the way to the ballpark, Coach gave us his usual scouting report: "These guys have power, and they have speed. It doesn't always show up. But when it does, look out. We have the same stuff, but you know I talk all the time about consistency. I'm almost a little worried about how easy we've had it this week.

"If it's tough tonight, don't be surprised. Don't panic. Dig deeper. Their pitcher has probably the best—no, not the best, but the fastest—fastball round. I'm talking ninety-five on a good day. His change is almost impossible to identify. But he has a tendency to lean on that pitch when he's behind in the count. So on the first pitch think fastball, then watch the count. Once in a while he'll try a curve. He shouldn't, though. If you are fortunate enough to see that pitch, chances are it's a hanger and killable."

There was a capacity crowd for the final. I looked around for Dad and Lisa and finally spotted them a few rows back behind the Runners' dugout. I waved, and they waved back. For just a few seconds I thought about how lucky I was to have a friend like Lisa.

We were the visiting team tonight, decided by a flip of the coin. So we batted first. The six-foot-six Tide pitcher, Brandon Becker, was as fast as advertised. Tonight was going to be a guessing game. With two out, Nellie guessed right and sent a change over the fence in left. So we were up 1–0.

Carson was the star he always thought he was. All of us on the team joked about Carson's ego. He was confident, which was good. You just didn't want to be the captive audience when he started talking about himself. But that night would fuel Carson's self-love for a long time. He was, for five innings, unhittable.

Scouting reports are helpful, but not so much for single, important games. The Tide were used to rolling behind Becker, and when Carson frustrated them they started to get nervous.

In the sixth we brought in our second run on a fielding error and led 2–0. With two outs in the eighth, Carson struck out the batter. At least we thought so, but the ump called a ball and kept him alive. Coach almost got thrown out for arguing. Umps get really defensive when they know they've blown a call.

On the next pitch the Tide batter homered. It was 2–1.

In the top of the eighth Becker was still burning them in. It would have been a fun batting exercise, trying to hit ninety-five, if we knew ninety-five was coming. But Becker's well-disguised change was around eighty. He struck out all three of our batters.

In the bottom of the eighth Carson walked the leadoff guy, who then stole second. He got the next batter on a grounder and the guy after that on an infield fly. But the next Tide batter wouldn't go gently. He took Carson to 3–2.

Carson has a good fastball—around eighty-five, with a sink on it. But the problem is that Carson thinks it's even better than it is. If you guess it's coming, you've got a good shot at golfing the ball into the wild blue yonder. When Carson started shaking off Nick's signals, we all knew what was coming, and so, apparently, did the Tide batter. One swing later, it was the Tide leading 3–2.

I was coming up fourth in the ninth, if it got to me. But then Nellie and Sammy went out and it was down to one—Gus. I think he was at the plate for five minutes, fouling off pitches, taking random time-outs, and doing everything he could to rattle the pitcher. Finally he walked. It was up to me to keep us alive.

I caught some motion among the spectators and looked up. It was Dad, next to Lisa, and he was sending signals. I hadn't seen Dad do this since I was maybe nine, but

I remembered all of them. The signal he was giving me from the seats was "Take!"

I don't know why, but I did. And the first pitch was a ball. The next pitch was obviously inside for ball two. I looked back at the stands to see Dad signaling "fastball." What the heck. I dug in and prepared for the heater.

I connected, and from the way it felt off the bat I wasn't surprised to see the ball clear the fence. The cheering was making me deaf as I crossed the plate. I pointed to where Dad was sitting and took in his grin. I'm not sure I'd ever felt so good about anything before.

The Tide led off the bottom of the ninth with a double. Carson struck out the next guy, but he walked the batter after him. We really needed a double play. But Carson was again shaking off Nick's signals. Finally Nick called a conference on the mound. Coach came out and all the infielders gathered around.

"What's going on?" Coach said.

I spoke up. "Carson, everyone knows you lean on your fastball. Shaking off Nick is a tell."

"Okay," Carson said to Coach. "What do you want?"

"Do what Nick asks you to do," Coach said.

The next batter was way ahead of Carson's curve and wound up striking out. The third guy, a pinch hitter, nailed it, but it went right to Darius in left. We were the champions.

When you win something big, you know there's a party in your future. And the Runners knew how to party. But instead of celebrating with the team, I ran up into the seats to Dad and Lisa.

Lisa just held me very tight for a minute. Dad had a comical shiner, but otherwise he was a happy man and, he told me, a proud father. I felt years older, and so much happier, than I had just a few weeks before.

ABOUT THE AUTHOR

Rick Jasper is a former middle school teacher and a long-time magazine editor and writer. A native of Kansas City, Missouri, he currently lives in Raleigh, North Carolina, with his daughter.

*"The road to the pros
starts here."*

LOOK FOR THESE
TITLES FROM THE

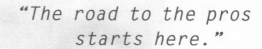

COLLECTION.

THE CATCH

When Danny makes "the catch," everyone seems interested in him. Girls text him, kids ask for autographs, and his highlight play even makes it on SportsCenter's Top Plays. A sports-gear executive tempts Danny with a big-money offer, and he decides to take advantage of his newfound fame. Danny agrees to wear the company's gear when he plays. But as his bank account gets bigger, so does his ego. Will Danny be able to keep his head in the game?

POWER HITTER

Sammy Perez has to make it to the big leagues. After his teammate's career-ending injury, the Roadrunners decided to play in a wood bat tournament to protect their pitchers. And while Sammy used to be a hotheaded, hard-hitting, home-run machine, he's now stuck in the slump of his life. Sammy thinks the wood bats are causing the problem, but his dad suggests that maybe he's not strong enough. Is Sammy willing to break the law and sacrifice his health to get an edge by taking performance-enhancing drugs? Can Sammy break out of his slump in time to get noticed by major-league scouts?

FORCED OUT

Zack Waddell's baseball IQ makes him one of the Roadrunners' most important players. When a new kid, Dustin, immediately takes their starting catcher's spot, Zack is puzzled. Dustin doesn't have the skills to be a starter. So Zack offers to help him with his swing in Dustin's swanky personal batting cages.

Zack accidentally overhears a conversation and figures out why Dustin is starting—and why the team is suddenly able to afford an expensive trip to a New York tournament. Will Zack's baseball instincts transfer off the field? Will the Roadrunners be able to stay focused when their team chemistry faces its greatest challenge yet?

THE PROSPECT

Nick Cosimo eats, breathes, and lives baseball. He's a place-hitting catcher, with a cannon for an arm and a calculator for a brain. Thanks to his keen eye, Nick is able to pick apart his opponents, taking advantage of their weaknesses. His teammates and coaches rely on his good instincts between the white lines. But when Nick spots a scout in the stands, everything changes. Will Nick alter his game plan to impress the scout enough to get drafted? Or will Nick put the team before himself?

OUT OF CONTROL

Carlos "Trip" Costas is a fiery shortstop with many talents and passions. His father is Julio Costas—yes, *the* Julio Costas, the famous singer. Unfortunately, Julio is also famous for being loud, controlling, and sometimes violent with Trip. Julio dreams of seeing his son play in the majors, but that's not what Trip wants.

When Trip decides to take a break from baseball to focus on his own music, his father loses his temper. He threatens to stop donating money to the team. Will the Roadrunners survive losing their biggest financial backer and their star shortstop? Will Trip have the courage to follow his dreams and not his father's?

HIGH HEAT

Pitcher Seth Carter had Tommy John surgery on his elbow in hopes of being able to throw harder. Now his fastball cuts through batters like a 90 mph knife through butter. But one day, Seth's pitch gets away from him. The *clunk* of the ball on the batter's skull still haunts Seth in his sleep and on the field. His arm doesn't feel like part of his body anymore, and he goes from being the ace everybody wanted to the pitcher nobody trusts. With the biggest game of the year on the line, can Seth come through for the team?

SOUTHSIDE HIGH

ARE YOU A SURVIVOR?

Check out all the books in the

SURVIVING SOUTH SIDE

collection.

Bad Deal

Fish hates having to take ADHD meds. They help him concentrate but also make him feel weird. So when a cute girl needs a boost to study for tests, Fish offers her one of his pills. Soon more kids want pills, and Fish likes the profits. To keep from running out, Fish finds a doctor who sells phony prescriptions. But suddenly the doctor is arrested. Fish realizes he needs to tell the truth. But will that cost him his friends?

Recruited

Kadeem is a star quarterback for Southside High. He is thrilled when college scouts seek him out. One recruiter even introduces him to a college cheerleader and gives him money to have a good time. But then officials start to investigate illegal recruiting. Will Kadeem decide to help their investigation, even though it means the end of the good times? What will it do to his chances of playing in college?

Benito Runs

Benito's father had been in Iraq for over a year. When he returns, Benito's family life is not the same. Dad suffers from PTSD—post-traumatic stress disorder—and yells constantly. Benito can't handle seeing his dad so crazy, so he decides to run away. Will Benny find a new life? Or will he learn how to deal with his dad—through good times and bad?

PLAN B

Lucy has her life planned: She'll graduate and join her boyfriend at college in Austin. She'll become a Spanish teacher, and of course they'll get married. So there's no reason to wait, right? They try to be careful, but Lucy gets pregnant. Lucy's plan is gone. How will she make the most difficult decision of her life?

BEATEN

Keah's a cheerleader and Ty's a football star, so they seem like the perfect couple. But when they have their first fight, Ty is beginning to scare Keah with his anger. Then after losing a game, Ty goes ballistic and hits Keah repeatedly. Ty is arrested for assault, but Keah still secretly meets up with Ty. How can Keah be with someone she's afraid of? What's worse—flinching every time your boyfriend gets angry or being alone?

Shattered Star

Cassie is the best singer at Southside and dreams of being famous. She skips school to try out for a national talent competition. But her hopes sink when she sees the line. Then a talent agent shows up, and Cassie is flattered to hear she has "the look" he wants. Soon she is lying and missing rehearsal to meet with him. And he's asking her for more each time. How far will Cassie go for her shot at fame?